MW00914964

The Wedding-Knell

by

Nathaniel Hawthorne

Rise of Douai

Copyright © 2013 Rise of Douai

ISBN-13: 978-1493698899

ISBN-10: 1493698893

Introduction

The Wedding-Knell is a short story by Nathaniel Hawthorne.

Nathaniel Hawthorne (born Nathaniel Hathorne; July 4, 1804 – May 19, 1864) was an American novelist and short story writer.

He was born in 1804 in Salem, Massachusetts to Nathaniel Hathorne and the former Elizabeth Clarke Manning. His ancestors include John Hathorne, the only judge involved in the Salem witch trials who never repented of his actions. Nathaniel later added a "w" to make his name "Hawthorne" in order to hide this relation. He entered Bowdoin College in 1821, was elected to Phi Beta Kappa in 1824, and graduated in 1825. Hawthorne published his first work, a novel titled Fanshawe, in 1828; he later tried to suppress it, feeling it was not equal to the standard of his later work. He published several short stories in various periodicals which he collected in 1837 as Twice-Told Tales. The next year, he became engaged to Sophia Peabody. He worked at a Custom House and joined Brook Farm, a transcendentalist community, before marrying Peabody in 1842. The couple moved to The Old Manse in Concord, Massachusetts, later moving to Salem, the Berkshires, then to The Wayside in Concord. The Scarlet Letter was published in 1850, followed by a succession of other novels. A political appointment took Hawthorne and family to Europe before their return to The Wayside in 1860.

Hawthorne died on May 19, 1864, and was survived by his wife and their three children.

Much of Hawthorne's writing centers on New England, many works featuring moral allegories with a Puritan inspiration. His fiction works are considered part of the Romantic movement and, more specifically, Dark romanticism. His themes often center on the inherent evil and sin of humanity, and his works often have moral messages and deep psychological complexity. His published works include novels, short stories, and a biography of his friend Franklin Pierce.

Hawthorne had a particularly close relationship with his publishers William Ticknor and James Thomas Fields. Hawthorne once told Fields, "I care more for your good opinion than for that of a host of critics". In fact, it was Fields who convinced Hawthorne to turn The Scarlet Letter into a novel rather than a short story. Ticknor handled many of Hawthorne's personal matters, including the purchase of cigars, overseeing financial accounts, and even purchasing clothes. Ticknor died with Hawthorne at his side in Philadelphia in 1864; Hawthorne was left, according to a friend, "apparently dazed".

The Wedding-Knell

There is a certain church in the city of New York which I have always regarded with peculiar interest, on account of a marriage there solemnized, under very singular circumstances, in my grandmother's girlhood. That venerable lady chanced to be a spectator of the scene, and ever after made it her favorite narrative. Whether the edifice now standing on the same site be the identical one to which she referred, I am not antiquarian enough to know; nor would it be worth while to correct myself, perhaps, of an agreeable error, by reading the date of its erection on the tablet over the door. It is a stately church, surrounded by an inclosure of the loveliest green, within which appear urns, pillars, obelisks, and other forms of monumental marble, the tributes of private affection, or more splendid memorials of historic dust. With such a place, though the tumult of the city rolls beneath its tower, one would be willing to connect some legendary interest.

The marriage might be considered as the result of an early engagement, though there had been two intermediate weddings on the lady's part, and forty years of celibacy on that of the gentleman. At sixty-five, Mr. Ellenwood was a shy, but not quite a secluded man; selfish, like all men who brood over their own hearts, yet manifesting on rare occasions a vein of generous sentiment; a scholar throughout life, though always an indolent one, because his studies had no definite object, either of public advantage or personal ambition; a gentleman, high bred and fastidiously delicate, yet sometimes requiring a considerable relaxation, in his behalf, of the common rules of society. In truth, there were so many anomalies in his character, and though shrinking with diseased sensibility from public notice, it had been his fatality so often to become the topic of the day, by some wild eccentricity of conduct, that people searched his lineage for an hereditary taint of insanity. But there was no need of this. His caprices had their origin in a mind that lacked the support of an engrossing purpose, and in feelings that preyed upon themselves for want of other food. If he were mad, it was the consequence, and not the cause, of an aimless and abortive life.

The widow was as complete a contrast to her third bridegroom, in everything but age, as can well be conceived. Compelled to relinquish her first engagement, she had been united to a man of twice her own years, to whom she became an exemplary wife, and by whose death she was left in possession of a splendid fortune. A southern gentleman, considerably younger than herself, succeeded to her hand, and carried her to Charleston, where, after many uncomfortable years, she found herself again a widow. It would have been singular, if any uncommon delicacy of feeling had survived through such a life as Mrs. Dabney's; it could not but be crushed and killed by her early disappointment, the cold duty of her first marriage, the dislocation of the heart's principles, consequent on a second union, and the unkindness of her southern husband, which had inevitably driven her to connect the idea of his death with that of her comfort. To be brief, she was that wisest, but unloveliest, variety of woman, a philosopher, bearing troubles of the heart with equanimity, dispensing with all that should have been her happiness, and making the best of what remained. Sage in most matters, the widow was perhaps the more amiable for the one frailty that made her ridiculous. Being childless, she could not remain beautiful by proxy, in the person of a daughter; she therefore refused to grow old and ugly, on any consideration; she struggled with Time, and held fast her roses in spite of him, till the venerable thief appeared to have relinquished the spoil, as not worth the trouble of acquiring it.

The approaching marriage of this woman of the world with such an unworldly man as Mr. Ellenwood was announced soon after Mrs. Dabney's return to her native city. Superficial observers, and deeper ones, seemed to concur in supposing that the lady must have borne no inactive part in arranging the affair; there were considerations of expediency which she would be far more likely to appreciate than Mr. Ellenwood; and there was just the specious phantom of sentiment and romance in this late union of two early lovers which sometimes makes a fool of a woman who has lost her true feelings among the accidents of life. All the wonder was, how the gentleman, with his lack of worldly wisdom and agonizing consciousness of ridicule, could have been induced to take a measure at once so prudent and so laughable. But while people talked the wedding-day arrived. The ceremony was to be solemnized according to the Episcopalian forms, and in open church, with a degree of publicity that attracted many spectators, who occupied the front seats of the galleries, and the pews near the altar and along the broad aisle. It had been arranged, or possibly it was the custom of the day, that the parties should proceed separately to church. By some accident the bridegroom was a little less punctual than the widow and her bridal attendants; with whose arrival, after this tedious, but necessary preface, the action of our tale may be said to commence.

The clumsy wheels of several old-fashioned coaches were heard, and the gentlemen and ladies composing the bridal party came through the church door with the sudden and gladsome effect of a burst of sunshine. The whole group, except the principal figure, was made up of youth and gayety. As they streamed up the broad aisle, while the pews and pillars seemed to brighten on either side, their steps were as buoyant as if they mistook the church for a ball-room, and were ready to dance hand in hand to the altar. So brilliant was the spectacle that few took notice of a singular phenomenon that had marked its entrance. At the moment when the bride's foot touched the threshold the bell swung heavily in the tower above her, and sent forth its deepest knell. The vibrations died away and returned with prolonged solemnity, as she entered the body of the church.

"Good heavens! what an omen," whispered a young lady to her lover.

"On my honor," replied the gentleman, "I believe the bell has the good taste to toll of its own accord. What has she to do with weddings? If you, dearest Julia, were approaching the altar the bell would ring out its merriest peal. It has only a funeral knell for her."

The bride and most of her company had been too much occupied with the bustle of entrance to hear the first boding stroke of the bell, or at least to reflect on the singularity of such a welcome to the altar. They therefore continued to advance with undiminished gayety. The gorgeous dresses of the time, the crimson velvet coats, the gold-laced hats, the hoop petticoats, the silk, satin, brocade, and embroidery, the buckles, canes, and swords, all displayed to the best advantage on persons suited to such finery, made the group appear more like a bright-colored picture than anything real. But by what perversity of taste had the artist represented his principal figure as so wrinkled and decayed, while yet he had decked her out in the brightest splendor of attire, as if the loveliest maiden had suddenly withered into age, and become a moral to the beautiful around her! On they went, however, and had glittered along about a third of the aisle, when another stroke of the bell seemed to fill the church with a visible gloom, dimming and obscuring the bright pageant, till it shone forth again as from a mist.

This time the party wavered, stopped, and huddled closer together, while a slight scream was heard from some of the ladies, and a confused whispering among the gentlemen. Thus tossing to and fro, they might have been fancifully compared to a splendid bunch of flowers, suddenly shaken by a puff of wind, which threatened to scatter the leaves of an old, brown, withered rose, on the same stalk with two dewy buds,-- such being the emblem of the widow between her fair young bridemaids. But her heroism was admirable. She had started with an irrepressible shudder, as if the stroke of the bell had fallen directly on her heart; then, recovering herself, while her attendants were yet in dismay, she took the lead, and paced calmly up the aisle. The bell continued to swing, strike, and vibrate, with the same doleful regularity as when a corpse is on its way to the tomb.

"My young friends here have their nerves a little shaken," said the widow, with a smile, to the clergyman at the altar. "But so many weddings have been ushered in with the merriest peal of the bells, and yet turned out unhappily, that I shall hope for better fortune under such different auspices."

"Madam," answered the rector, in great perplexity, "this strange occurrence brings to my mind a marriage sermon of the famous Bishop Taylor, wherein he mingles so many thoughts of mortality and future woe, that, to speak somewhat after his own rich style, he seems to hang the bridal chamber in black, and cut the wedding garment out of a coffin pall. And it has been the custom of divers nations to infuse something of sadness into their marriage ceremonies, so to keep death in mind while contracting that engagement which is life's chiefest business. Thus we may draw a sad but profitable moral from this funeral knell."

But, though the clergyman might have given his moral even a keener point, he did not fail to dispatch an attendant to inquire into the mystery, and stop those sounds, so dismally appropriate to such a marriage. A brief space elapsed, during which the silence was broken only by whispers, and a few suppressed titterings, among the wedding party and the spectators, who, after the first shock, were disposed to draw an ill-natured merriment from the affair. The young have less charity for aged follies than the old for those of youth. The widow's glance was observed to wander, for an instant, towards a window of the church, as if searching for the time-worn marble that she had dedicated to her first husband; then her eyelids dropped over their faded orbs, and her thoughts were drawn irresistibly to another grave. Two buried men, with a voice at her ear, and a cry afar off, were calling her to lie down beside them. Perhaps, with momentary truth of feeling, she thought how much happier had been her fate, if, after years of bliss, the bell were now tolling for her funeral, and she were followed to the grave by the old affection of her earliest lover, long her husband. But why had she returned to him, when their cold hearts shrank from each other's embrace?

Still the death-bell tolled so mournfully, that the sunshine seemed to fade in the air. A whisper, communicated from those who stood nearest the windows, now spread through the church; a hearse, with a train of several coaches, was creeping along the street, conveying some dead man to the churchyard, while the bride awaited a living one at the altar. Immediately after, the footsteps of the bridegroom and his friends were heard at the door. The widow looked down the aisle, and clinched the arm of one of her bridemaids in her bony hand with such unconscious violence, that the fair girl trembled.

"You frighten me, my dear madam!" cried she. "For Heaven's sake, what is the matter?"

"Nothing, my dear, nothing," said the widow; then, whispering close to her ear, "There is a foolish fancy that I cannot get rid of. I am expecting my bridegroom to come into the church, with my first two husbands for groomsmen!"

"Look, look!" screamed the bridemaid. "What is here? The funeral!"

As she spoke, a dark procession paced into the church. First came an old man and women, like chief mourners at a funeral, attired from head to foot in the deepest black, all but their pale features and hoary hair; he leaning on a staff, and supporting her decrepit form with his nerveless arm. Behind appeared another, and another pair, as aged, as black, and mournful as the

12

first. As they drew near, the widow recognized in every face some trait of former friends, long forgotten, but now returning, as if from their old graves, to warn her to prepare a shroud; or, with purpose almost as unwelcome, to exhibit their wrinkles and infirmity, and claim her as their companion by the tokens of her own decay. Many a merry night had she danced with them, in youth. And now, in joyless age, she felt that some withered partner should request her hand, and all unite, in a dance of death, to the music of the funeral bell.

While these aged mourners were passing up the aisle, it was observed that, from pew to pew, the spectators shuddered with irrepressible awe, as some object, hitherto concealed by the intervening figures, came full in sight. Many turned away their faces; others kept a fixed and rigid stare; and a young girl giggled hysterically, and fainted with the laughter on her lips. When the spectral procession approached the altar, each couple separated, and slowly diverged, till, in the centre, appeared a form, that had been worthily ushered in with all this gloomy pomp, the death knell, and the funeral. It was the bridegroom in his shroud!

No garb but that of the grave could have befitted such a deathlike aspect; the eyes, indeed, had the wild gleam of a sepulchral lamp; all else was fixed in the stern calmness which old men wear in the coffin. The corpse stood motionless, but addressed the widow in accents that seemed to melt into the clang of the bell, which fell heavily on the air while he spoke.

"Come, my bride!" said those pale lips, "the hearse is ready. The sexton stands waiting for us at the door of the tomb. Let us be married; and then to our coffins!"

How shall the widow's horror be represented? It gave her the ghastliness of a dead man's bride. Her youthful friends stood apart, shuddering at the mourners, the shrouded bridegroom, and herself; the whole scene expressed, by the strongest imagery, the vain struggle of the gilded vanities of this world, when opposed to age, infirmity, sorrow, and death. The awe-struck silence was first broken by the clergyman.

"Mr. Ellenwood," said he, soothingly, yet with somewhat of authority, "you are not well. Your mind has been agitated by the unusual circumstances in which you are placed. The ceremony must be deferred. As an old friend, let me entreat you to return home."

"Home! yes, but not without my bride," answered he, in the same hollow accents. "You deem this mockery; perhaps madness. Had I bedizened my aged and broken frame with scarlet and embroidery--had I forced my withered lips to smile at my dead heart--that might have been mockery, or madness. But now, let young and old declare, which of us has come hither without a wedding garment, the bridegroom or the bride!"

He stepped forward at a ghostly pace, and stood

beside the widow, contrasting the awful simplicity of his shroud with the glare and glitter in which she had arrayed herself for this unhappy scene. None, that beheld them, could deny the terrible strength of the moral which his disordered intellect had contrived to draw.

"Cruel! cruel!" groaned the heart-stricken bride.

"Cruel!" repeated he; then, losing his deathlike composure in a wild bitterness: "Heaven judge which of us has been cruel to the other! In youth you deprived me of my happiness, my hopes, my aims; you took away all the substance of my life, and made it a dream without reality enough even to grieve at--with only a pervading gloom, through which I walked wearily, and cared not whither. But after forty years, when I have built my tomb, and would not give up the thought of resting there--nor not for such a life as we once pictured--you call me to the altar. At your summons I am here. But other husbands have enjoyed your youth, your beauty, your warmth of heart, and all that could be termed your life. What is there for me but your decay and death? And therefore I have bidden these funeral friends, and bespoken the sexton's deepest knell, and am come, in my shroud, to wed you, as with a burial service, that we may join our hands at the door of the sepulchre, and enter it together."

It was not frenzy; it was not merely the drunkenness of strong emotion, in a heart unused to it, that now wrought upon the bride. The stern lesson of the day had done its work; her worldliness was gone. She seized the bridegroom's hand.

"Yes!" cried she. "Let us wed, even at the door of the sepulchre! My life is gone in vanity and emptiness. But at its close there is one true feeling. It has made me what I was in youth; it makes me worthy of you. Time is no more for both of us. Let us wed for Eternity!"

With a long and deep regard, the bridegroom looked into her eyes, while a tear was gathering in his own. How strange that gush of human feeling from the frozen bosom of a corpse! He wiped away the tears even with his shroud.

"Beloved of my youth," said he, "I have been wild. The despair of my whole lifetime had returned at once, and maddened me. Forgive; and be forgiven. Yes; it is evening with us now; and we have realized none of our morning dreams of happiness. But let us join our hands before the altar as lovers whom adverse circumstances have separated through life, yet who meet again as they are leaving it, and find their earthly affection changed into something holy as religion. And what is Time, to the married of Eternity?"

Amid the tears of many, and a swell of exalted sentiment, in those who felt aright, was solemnized the union of two immortal souls. The train of withered mourners, the hoary bridegroom in his shroud, the pale features of the aged bride, and the death-bell tolling through the whole, till its deep voice overpowered the marriage words, all marked the funeral of earthly hopes. But as the ceremony proceeded, the organ, as if stirred by the sympathies of this impressive scene, poured forth an anthem, first mingling with the dismal knell, then rising to a loftier strain, till the soul looked down upon its woe. And when the awful rite was finished, and with cold hand in cold hand, the Married of Eternity withdrew, the organ's peal of solemn triumph drowned the Wedding Knell.

THE END

RISE OF DOUAI

RISE OF DOUAI

TWITTER : @RISEOFDOUAI

- AN IDIOT'S GUIDE TO: BEE HUNTING BY JOHN LOCKARD, EDITED BY ARSALAN AHMED (2012)(PAPERBACK) ISBN-10: 1478383550

- THE RISE OF DOUAI BY ARSALAN AHMED (2012)(PAPERBACK) ISBN-10: 1479267783

- THE RICHEST MAN IN BABYLON BY GEORGE S. CLASON (2012) (PAPERBACK) ISBN-10: 1479377341

- THINK AND GROW RICH BY NAPOLEON HILL (2012) (PAPERBACK) ISBN-10: 1480061638

- AS A MAN THINKETH BY MR JAMES ALLEN (2012) (PAPERBACK) ISBN-10: 1480088161
- HOW TO ANALYZE PEOPLE ON

SIGHT BY ELSIE BENEDICT (PAPERBACK) ISBN-10: 1480081272

- THE ART OF WAR BY MR SUN TZU (PAPERBACK) ISBN-10: 1480082007
- MACBETH BY MR WILLIAM SHAKESPEARE (PAPERBACK) ISBN-10: 1480060682
- A CHRISTMAS CAROL BY MR CHARLES DICKENS ISBN-10: 1481194755
- CREATING CAPITAL: MONEY-MAKING AS AN AIM IN BUSINESS BY MR FREDRICK L LIPMAN ISBN-10: 1481158996
- GETTING GOLD: A PRACTICAL TREATISE FOR PROSPECTORS, MINERS, AND STUDENTS BY MR JOSEPH COLIN FRANCIS JOHNSON ISBN-10: 1481090984
- THE INTERPRETATION OF DREAMS BY MR SIGMUND FREUD ISBN-10: 1481134558
- THE COMMUNIST MANIFESTO BY MR KARL MARX AND MR FRIDRICK ENGLES ISBN-10:

1480112445

- THE PRINCE BY MR NICCOLO MACHIAVELLI ISBN-10: 1480119601
- THE WAY TO WEALTH BY MR BENJAMIN FRANKLIN ISBN-10: 1480099651
- THE ART OF MONEY GETTING - OR GOLDEN RULES FOR MAKING MONEY (SUCCESS PRINCIPLES) BY MR PHINEAS TAYLOR BARNUM ISBN-10: 1480138622

Twitter : **@RiseofDouai**

34034928R00016

Made in the USA
Lexington, KY
20 July 2014